ALSO BY BARBARA PARK

BY BARBARA PARK

ALFRED A. KNOPF

NEW YORK

THIS IS A BORZOI BOOK PUBLISHED BY ALFRED A. KNOPF, INC.
Copyright © 1993 by Barbara Park
Jacket art copyright © 1993 by Paul Bachem

Library of Congress Cataloging-in-Publication Data
Park, Barbara.
Dear God, help! Love, Earl / by Barbara Park.
p.   cm.
Summary: Tired of being pushed around by the class bully, Earl and two
friends devise the perfect revenge.
ISBN 0-679-83431-1 (trade) — ISBN 0-679-93431-6 (lib. bdg.)
[1. Bullies—Fiction. 2. Schools—Fiction.] I. Title.
PZ7.P2197De 1993 [Fic]—dc20 92-20909

Manufactured in the United States of America
10 9 8 7 6 5 4 3 2 1

Contents

Death wears surfer shorts

Death is in my P.E. class.

I know him personally. He has brown hair and freckles and he wears surfer shorts.

A lot of people think that death wears a black hooded robe and has long white bony fingers. But that's only in the movies. In real life, death has a fairly decent tan, and he bites his nails right down to the nubs.

He's got a name, too. Death's name is Eddie McFee.

I met him the first week of school this year. No one introduced us or anything. He was sitting in the first row of the baseball bleachers, and when I walked past, he tripped me.

I don't mean I just stumbled over his foot, either. 'Cause when Eddie McFee trips you, he knocks your feet totally out from under you. And you go crashing down hard. Right on your can.

A whole lot of kids started laughing. But not Eddie. He just leaned back in the bleachers, folded his arms, and watched me real serious-like. You know, like I was some kind of lab rat or something.

My face turned beet-red. It felt hot, too. Embarrassingly hot.

"Ha ha. Very funny," I muttered.

Eddie didn't smile. "Oh, come on, Tubby," he said. "You're just trying to be nice. It wasn't *that* funny."

My stomach knotted up tight as a drum when I heard him call me Tubby. *That's not my name!* I wanted to shout. *My name is Earl Wilber! And I would appreciate it if you would use it!*

But shouting something like that would have been really gutsy. And I'm not the gutsy type. I mean, I have a few guts, but mostly I just use them for digestion.

Besides, after you've spent a whole lifetime listening to kids make fun of the way you look, you kind of learn to accept it, you know? You learn to keep your mouth shut, too. 'Cause if you don't, it only makes things worse.

Like one time in first grade this kid named John Paul Potter called me Miss Piggy during recess.

And it made me feel so sick inside I didn't know what to do. So finally I walked over to him and I said, "Sticks and stones will break my bones, but names will never hurt me."

That's when the chase began—John Paul and about four hundred of his friends started chasing me all over the playground. Some of them even had lassos, which were actually jump ropes I think. But still, a loop is a loop, you know?

Then Gloria Biddles lassoed my foot, and down I went into the grass and dirt. And I started to wheeze so bad I had to use my squeezy nose drops and my mouth inhaler.

The next thing I knew, John Paul Potter and his friends had formed a circle around me and were singing, "The cheese stands alone . . . the cheese stands alone . . . hi-ho the derry-o, the cheese stands alone."

Only they didn't exactly say "cheese."

They said "wheeze."

"The *wheeze* stands alone," they sang.

I remember closing my eyes and wishing that the ground would open right up and swallow me down to the middle of the earth. Because that way I would never have to see those mean kids again. Or hear their teasing voices. Or their hateful, mocking laughter.

Except the playground didn't open up that day.

In fact, the bell took so long to ring I was positive it must be broken.

But I can tell you one thing for sure. By the time I got back to my own desk, I knew that I would *never* try to stand up for myself again. Not *ever*.

Besides, if you're talking about standing up to a kid like Eddie McFee, you're talking about instant death.

At first I couldn't understand why he hated me so much. But now that I've had some time to think about it, I've decided that bullies like Eddie have a little part of their brain missing. It's the part where their compassion is supposed to be.

I mean, I know I'm on the chubby side. And I'm wheezy. And I have an unusual cowlick. But there's cool stuff about me, too. Invisible cool stuff. Like I'm a good friend, I think. And I'm kind to animals. That's cool, right?

Last spring I even stayed up for an entire weekend feeding a baby bird that had fallen out of its nest. But then on Monday morning my mother made me go to school. And when I got home that afternoon my cat, Chuck, was parading proudly around with my bird in his mouth. All dead. Like some sick prize he had won at a ghoulie carnival.

It made me cry for a really long time. I buried him in a box lined with flowers. I even made a cross out of some twigs and junk I found on the ground.

Not that Eddie McFee would care about that side of me. To him I'm just somebody to pick on.

You should have seen the way his eyes would dance around when he would get me alone in P.E. class. Then he'd either trip me or bang my head into the lockers. Or worse.

I didn't tell anybody about it, though. Not even my best friend, Maxie Zuckerman. Let's face it, there are some things just too humiliating to admit.

But unfortunately, Maxie found out anyway. One day he accidentally walked into the bathroom while Eddie was flushing my head down the toilet.

"Oops! Pardon me! My mistake, Ed," he apologized quickly as he backed right out again.

I didn't really blame Maxie for that. He only weighs about sixty pounds, so trying to come to my rescue would have been a suicide mission. And anyhow, as soon as Eddie had left the bathroom, Maxie rushed right back in to help me.

"You've got to tell the coach about this," he insisted. "I mean it, Earl. You've just *got* to."

I shook my head. "I don't 'got to' do anything, Max," I told him. "Forget it, okay? Just pretend it never happened."

Maxie's mouth practically dropped on the floor. "Pretend it never happened? Are you serious? I can't just pre—"

"Yes, you can!" I shouted at him. "I said I'm not telling anybody *anything*. Not Coach Rah. Not my mother. Not *anybody*. Do you know what Eddie McFee would do to me if I ratted on him? Huh? He would pound me into bone meal and serve me to his dog for Thanksgiving dinner. He's already explained it to me in great detail. I'm going to be served as a special dessert treat right after the table scraps. So just forget what you saw, okay? This is none of your beeswax."

After that, I slicked back my hair, which was still wet from the toilet, and left.

And—right or wrong—I never squealed on Eddie McFee.

I did try hiding from him one time, though. I mean, you just sort of owe it to your body to try hiding at least once, I think.

I got to the gym early that day and squeezed behind one of the tumbling mats hanging on the wall. But unfortunately Eddie found me right away. He lifted up the mat and gave me this grin that sent chills up my spine.

"Boo," he said quietly.

My upper lip quivered as I tried to smile. "Um, well, yes, boo to you, too, Ed," I said.

Quick as a flash, he reached in, grabbed my arm, and yanked me out as hard as he could. After that, he marched me into the boys' locker room and shoved me against the cinder-block wall. My head hit the wall pretty hard, too. I didn't cry or anything. But I wanted to.

"Quit it, Eddie," I blurted, surprising myself. "Why can't you just leave me alone? What did I ever do to make you hate me so much?"

For a split second Eddie looked totally puzzled. "*Hate* you? I don't hate you, fatboy," he replied, sounding almost sincere. Then he grinned that chilling grin again and pulled me up right next to his face. "You and me, we just have *fun* together, that's all."

A few seconds later I was in a headlock and the two of us were running all over the floor. "See? Isn't this fun, fatso?" he said, laughing meanly.

Just then some of my book club money came flying out of my shirt pocket. And when it hit the floor, I got an idea that seemed so great it was almost like a miracle!

"Wait!" I yelled out. "Hold it!" Then somehow I managed to pull out of the headlock and began scooping up my money as fast as I could.

"Here, Ed!" I said, shoving four quarters into his hands. "Wow! What a great idea I'm having here! Look at this! I'm giving you the money I brought to buy a book with! Get it? I'm *paying* you to stop hurting me!"

For a moment Eddie just stared at the money in his hands. Then all of a sudden his whole face lit up. "Hey, you know what? You just might have something here, Tubs," he agreed.

He put my quarters into his pocket and jingled them around a little bit. "Yup. It looks like you and me have just made ourselves a deal."

So that was pretty much that. From then on, that became our "little arrangement," I guess you'd call it. Every Wednesday morning before P.E. began, I would give Eddie McFee a dollar, and he wouldn't bother me for one whole week.

Seven *entire* days! At first it just seemed so perfect, you know?

Only as it turned out, there was one small problem with our "little arrangement" which I hadn't really thought of. Because the trouble with money is, unless you come from a very rich family, sooner or later it runs out.

And I don't come from a very rich family.

To be specific, my mother is a checkout clerk at Milo's Meat Market. That's the person who stands at the cash register and takes your money.

I used to think that she got to keep all the money in her register. But I was mistaken. She gets seven dollars and fifty cents an hour. Period.

My father sends child-support money every month, but he's not rich either. He and my mom got divorced when I was three. Then he moved back to England, which is where he was born.

I think I'm supposed to miss him, but I don't. He's an okay guy and all, but my mother and I have a lot more in common than me and my father. Like we don't call our oatmeal "porridge." And we almost never use words like "ducky" and "jolly good."

Also, my father calls his umbrella a bumbershoot. I mean, how can you feel close to a man like that?

Anyway, since Mom doesn't make that much, the only money I get comes from Christmas and birthdays and junk. I keep it hidden in a money sock in the back of my underwear drawer. That's what I was paying Eddie with.

But even though I knew my savings wouldn't last forever, it took me a while before I finally checked to see how much I had left. Then—one night when I was getting my money for P.E. the next day—I turned my money sock inside out and started counting the dollars that fell to the floor.

"One . . . two . . ."

I waited patiently, but nothing else came out.

"Two?" I gasped in disbelief, gazing at the empty sock. "No! There *has* to be more than two dollars left! There were at least nine in there when I started!"

My stomach knotted tight as a drum and little sweat drops started to pop out all over my forehead.

Oh, my God, I'm going to die, I thought. *After two more payments my money will be gone and Eddie is going to pulverize me.*

I crawled into bed and stared up at my ceiling like a dead man. Then in desperation I raised my hand in the air and quietly began to pray.

"Uh, 'scuse me, God?" I began politely. "It's Earl Wilber here again. Remember me? I'm the one who asked you to kill that kid in my P.E. class a few weeks ago?

"Okay . . . well, apparently you didn't feel right about that or something. And I respect that, I guess. But see, now my money sock is almost flat, so I really need to ask you one more favor.

"I *have* to be sick tomorrow, God. Seriously. I only have two dollars left to last me until my Christmas money comes in. And so you've got to get me out of P.E. tomorrow. That's not asking too much, is it? I mean, all I really need is a little rash or a fever or something. Or maybe one of those twenty-four-hour stomach flu things would be good.

"But whatever it is, please remember . . . it has to be an illness that my mother can either see, or measure with a thermometer. Like don't just give me a headache, or else she'll hand me a couple of Tylenol and I'll be at school so fast it'll make your head spin.

"Okay. Well, I guess that's about it, God. I'll let you get back to whatever you were doing. Meanwhile, I'll be waiting right here in my bed. So feel free to infect me with something whenever you get the chance.

"This is Earl Wilber, thanking you in advance.

"Over and out."

Nosy Rosie and other pains

The next morning I was fine. Seriously. I had never felt better in my life. No temperature. No rash. No nothing.

This time I didn't even bother raising my hand. I just looked up at my ceiling and frowned. "Okay, I realize you're busy, God. But geez, even Federal Express can deliver by ten o'clock the next day."

"Earl!" screeched my mother from down the hall. "Who are you talking to? It's late! Are you dressed yet?"

My mother has ears as big as all outdoors. Also, her morning voice sounds like fingernails scratching across a chalkboard.

"I'm almost ready!" I fibbed, quickly pulling on my sweatshirt.

I probably would have been more upset about having to go to school. But during the night, I had come up with a backup plan to get out of P.E. Even when you're counting on God to infect you, it's always good to have a backup plan, I think.

Mine was the nurse's office. I decided that if I didn't wake up sick, I would go to school, fake an ankle injury, and spend the day at Nurse Klonski's. It would be tricky and all. But it was definitely worth a try.

I'd still take my dollar to school, of course. I mean, just in case my backup plan failed, I sure didn't want to have to face Eddie McFee empty-handed.

In fact just the thought of it made my stomach so queasy I needed a dose of Pepto-Bismol. Then I had two Rolaids for that burning sensation, and I left for Maxie's house.

Since Maxie lives right across from school, me and our friend Rosie Swanson always meet him on his porch and walk the rest of the way together.

The three of us only met at the beginning of the year. But we're already best friends. That's because we're all kind of oddballs, I think.

Take Maxie, for instance. Even though he's real

scrawny, he's got the biggest brain in the entire school. Like he's never gotten anything below an A+ in his entire life. His hobby is reading the dictionary. I'm serious. He finds weird words in there, and then he adds them to his vocabulary. It's not normal. But it doesn't scare me as much as it used to.

As for Rosie, well, she's kind of the snoopy, tattletale type. Also, her grandfather used to be a cop, so she's always trying to force you to cross at crosswalks and junk like that. Maxie and I still like her a lot, though. Maxie says she's prudent and undaunting, whatever that means.

Anyway, as soon as I turned the corner for Maxie's house that morning, I looked down and saw the dollar bill creeping out of my jacket pocket.

"Oh geez," I said right out loud. The *last* thing I needed was for Rosie to start asking a bunch of questions about why I was bringing a dollar to school. I mean, paying Eddie to not beat me up was degrading enough. But if my friends ever found out about it, I'd die of humiliation.

Luckily I grabbed the dollar just as Rosie came running up beside me. Then I quick hid the money in my fist so she couldn't see it.

"Let's go, Earl," she said, rushing past me.

"We're late this morning. If we don't run, we're going to get tardy slips. Come on! Hustle!"

I hate it when people tell me to hustle. In the first place, my legs rub together when I run. And in the second place, I think everyone should be the boss of their own speed.

"Hustle yourself," I muttered as I kept right on walking.

But as usual, Rosie wouldn't take no for an answer, and she ran back and grabbed my hand to pull me.

Unfortunately, it was the hand with the dollar bill.

"Hey! What's in your fist, Earl? Is that money sticking out of there? What are you bringing money to school for? Is the PTA selling those big brownies you love again?"

I didn't answer.

Rosie kept at it. "Come on, tell me. Why are you bringing money to school?"

"Nosy," I said. "Nosy Rosie."

"Earl!" she demanded.

"It's for none of your beeswax, that's what it's for," I told her.

By now we were almost to Maxie's house. He was sitting on the porch step waiting for us.

"Hey, Max!" shouted Rosie. "Earl's got some

money in his fist, and he won't tell me what it's for!"

Maxie waited till I got a little closer. Then he raised one eyebrow like he was Sherlock Holmes or someone. "Oh?" he replied.

"*Oh* yourself," I snapped. "Geez, what's wrong with you guys, anyway? I brought a dollar to school. Big dumb deal. It's just for an emergency, okay? Haven't your mothers ever told you to carry money in case of an emergency?"

Rosie took a second to think it over. "Mine hasn't," she said. "She taught me CPR and the Heimlich maneuver. But she never said anything about carrying money."

Maxie shook his head. "Mine hasn't either. In case of an emergency, I'm supposed to call my uncle Murray. The personal injury lawyer."

He reached into his book bag and pulled out one of his uncle Murray's business cards. It said:

IF YOU'RE HURT
AND LIFE'S NO FUN,
CALL ME
AND WE'LL SUE SOMEONE.

Murray Zuckerman
Personal Injury Attorney
(602) 555–3546

"He's an excellent lawyer," Maxie added proudly. "He can make you think you've been injured even if you haven't."

I rolled my eyes and started across the cross-walk. That's when the school bell started to ring.

Rosie took off like a rocket. The thought of being tardy totally freaks her out. Maxie started to hurry, too.

"See you in P.E., Earl," he called.

Even though the two of us are in different rooms, all the fifth-grade boys have P.E. together on Wednesday and Friday mornings.

I crossed my fingers. "Not if I can help it," I said under my breath.

A few minutes later I was standing in the hall-way outside Nurse Klonski's office. I could see her sitting at her desk rubbing her temples. Nurse Klonski is one of those school officials who al-ways seems to have a headache.

"Ow!" I said, getting her attention. Then I made a pained face and slowly began limping into the room.

"Ouch! Ow!" I cried again.

But instead of coming to my rescue, Nurse Klonski lowered her head to her desktop and covered up with her arms. "No. Please, Mr. Wil-ber," I heard her mumble. "Not you. Not today."

I'm not exactly what you'd call one of Nurse

Klonski's favorite people. I'm the only kid I know who's ever gotten a comment from the nurse on his report card. It said:

EARL MAKES TOO MANY UNNECESSARY VISITS.
—N.K.

I grimaced in pain. "I'm sorry to bother you, Nurse Klonski," I said, sounding as weak and pathetic as I could. "But I fell on my ankle coming up the school steps this morning. And I think it might be broken."

Boy, that sure got her attention.

"What?" she blurted. "Why didn't you say so, Earl?" Then she ran around the desk, helped me to the cot, and quickly started to remove my shoe and sock.

"*Ow! Ow! That kills!*" I yelled.

Nurse Klonski pulled her hand away. "But I barely even touched you," she said.

"I know. It just hurts, that's all," I whined.

Gently she tried one more time.

"*Ow! Stop!*" I screamed louder than before.

By now the nurse seemed seriously worried. "We'll have to get this x-rayed," she said, frowning. "Do you have school insurance?"

I shrugged weakly. "I don't know if my mom had the money to buy it this year."

I paused for effect. "Maybe we could just prop

18

my foot up on some pillows for a while and see if it gets better on its own. I don't mind lying here if it'll save my mother an x-ray bill, Mrs. Klonski. Really I don't."

Staring down at my ankle, I sighed glumly. "Darn it. I guess this probably means I'll have to miss P.E. for a while, doesn't it? I mean, geez, I might not be able to go for weeks. Or even months, possibly," I observed.

I paused again. "You know, as long as we're on the subject of P.E., maybe you should go ahead and write an excuse to Coach Rah to get me out of class today. 'Cause like even if a miracle happened and my ankle was all better by ten o'clock, I still don't think I should put any weight on it for a while. Do you?"

At first Nurse Klonski didn't answer me. She just kind of stood there looking at me real curious-like. Then all of a sudden she seemed to relax a little bit.

"You know something, Earl?" she said. "Now that I think about it, you might be right about the x-ray. Why don't we forget about that for a while, and I'll go get some pillows to elevate your foot. Don't move, okay?"

She went to her office door and started into the hall.

That's when I heard her gasp in horror.

"*Oh, my stars in heaven! What a hideous*

19

creature. *Run, everyone! Run for your lives!*" she exclaimed.

Frantically she dashed back into the office and slammed the door. Then she leaned against it with all her weight.

I was at her side in an instant! I'm not kidding. In less than a second I was jumping up and down trying to peek through the little window at the top of the door.

"WHAT'S OUT THERE? WHAT IS IT? WHAT IS IT?" I yelled.

Still leaning against the door, Nurse Klonski turned her head in my direction. Then slowly she lowered her eyes down my body until they were focused on my perfectly fine ankle.

I stopped jumping. But it was too late.

When Nurse Klonski finally raised her head again, she was grinning like the cat in *Alice in Wonderland*. I mean it. Her face looked weirder than anything.

I felt myself begin to tremble. Nervously I pulled at my collar and pointed to the hall. "Uh . . . just for the record . . . there's nothing really out there, is there?" I managed.

Nurse Klonski's grin widened. She shook her head no.

"This was . . . this was just a little trick, wasn't it?" I went on.

Silently she nodded.

I swallowed hard. Slowly I began groping for the doorknob behind me. Then without taking my eyes off her, I gently pulled the door open and began backing out.

"Have a nice day," I said softly.

As soon as I was safely in the hall, I shut the door behind me and collapsed in relief on the floor.

A minute later I heard a tapping sound. When I looked up, Nurse Klonski's eyes were peering down at me from her little window.

She waved her fingers.

I won't be going back.

Mrs. Mota dismissed us for P.E. at ten o'clock. I still remember how sick I felt walking to the gym.

As usual, Eddie McFee was waiting for me in the boys' bathroom. That's where we always made our "exchange."

I took one look at him and blessed myself. I'm not Catholic, but I'm pretty sure anybody can bless themselves. Like the Catholics don't own it or anything.

Eddie gave me one of his normal friendly greetings. "You got the money, Chunky?" he asked.

Quickly I pulled out my dollar. "Yeah, sure,

Eddie. Here it is," I said, handing it over. "Only before you go, there's something I sort of need to talk to you about, okay?"

The muscles in Eddie's face tightened. "Like what kind of something?" he asked.

I took a deep breath. Then I started explaining all about how broke I was. And how maybe if we lowered the payments to fifty cents a week, my money would last twice as long.

"This is only a temporary problem, Ed," I assured him. "I'll be getting more money at Christmas. So what do you say? Could we lower the payments for a while, do you think?"

Eddie didn't have to think at all. He just grabbed me by the shirt and pushed me against the wall. Then he put his foot on my stomach, and he pressed so hard I thought I would split in two.

"This is a joke, isn't it, Jumbo?" he growled.

Somehow I managed to nod.

Eddie sneered. "Good, fatboy," he said. "That's real good. 'Cause guess what? If I don't keep gettin' my money, I'm going to get real mad. And if I get real mad, I might do somethin' to you that doesn't feel so good. You know, somethin' like *this*."

Before I knew it, Eddie had grabbed hold of my ears and was practically lifting me off the ground. I'm not èxaggerating either. It hurt worse than anything I remember. Like he was ripping them right off my head or something.

My eyes filled with tears.

A second later one of the tears ran down my cheek.

Eddie started to grin. "Oooooh. What's da twouble? Is da widdle baby stawting to cwy?" he teased.

At last he let go of my ears and shoved me back into the wall. He pointed his finger in my face.

"Don't ever joke around like that again, Tubby," he warned. "Do you understand? Not *ever*."

Finally he stormed off.

I hurried to the sink and turned on the water as loud as it would go. Then I finished crying as softly as I could.

Torture

I was still trying to brush Eddie's dirty footprint off the front of my shirt when Maxie came into the gym.

He squinted and stared at the mark. "Who danced on your stomach?" he wanted to know.

I turned away from him. "Nobody, okay? Never mind."

Luckily, just then Coach Rah came bounding into the gym and gave a loud blast on his whistle. "Kickball today, gentlemen!" he shouted enthusiastically. Then he crossed his muscular arms and waited while we all sat down in the bleachers.

"Today's captains are Paulie Little and Leon Lucas," the coach boomed. *"Paulie? Leon? Get down here and choose up sides, men!"*

Paulie and Leon hurried to the middle of the floor and started scanning the stands to see who they wanted to pick. But even though I was sitting up straight and tall, their eyes passed over me like I was the invisible man.

I always get picked last. *Always.* Ever since kindergarten, it's been the same thing. I sit in the bleachers as the captains call out names. And one by one the rows begin to empty.

Until pretty soon there's only a few of us left.

There's six . . .

Then there's four . . .

And then there's just me and one other kid.

That's when I cross my fingers and pray that this time—just this once—I won't get picked last.

Then the other kid gets chosen.

And there's just me.

Sitting in the stands all alone.

It's like I'm wearing a giant sign that says I SUCK.

And it's torture. Absolute total torture.

I mean, I know there are other tortures that are worse. Like I wouldn't want to be lowered into a pit full of snakes. And one time my mother made me watch that entire *Nutcracker* thing on PBS.

But what makes it even harder is that Eddie McFee is always chosen first. *Always.*

Death is an excellent athlete. Real coordinated and all. Like you should see the cool way he strolls onto the floor after he gets picked. Even with rubber soles on, he practically glides.

This time Paulie Little won the toss.

"Eddie McFee," he said in a flash.

"Gee. What a surprise," I mumbled to Max.

I heaved a big sigh and slumped over. "It's not my fault that I'm not a good athlete, you know. I mean, geez, my father's from England. They don't even *have* sports over there."

Suddenly I felt myself getting annoyed. "Did you know my father's name is Cecil? Cecil Halliwell Wilber III. Yeah, boy. That really sounds like an athlete's name, doesn't it?"

My voice got louder. "Guess what his favorite sport is, Max?"

Maxie gave me the "shh" sign. But I was suddenly so annoyed with my father that I couldn't seem to control my volume.

"Come on. Guess," I insisted. "This'll really kill you."

Maxie reached over and tried to cover my mouth. But he wasn't in time.

"DARTS!" I spouted. "The man plays darts, Max! He's even got his own special little dart box that he carries around with him! Can you believe that?"

I made my voice sound British. "He says it's JOLLY GOOD FUN!"

Coach Rah glared up at me from the floor. "Hey, Prince Charles? You wanna put a sock in it, son?" he shouted.

All at once the gym exploded in loud, uncontrollable laughter.

Sweat poured out of my forehead like it was a faucet. God! Why did it always have to be like this? I closed my eyes and plugged my ears to block out the roar. But I knew it wouldn't work. 'Cause no matter how hard you press on your ears, you can never keep the laughter out of your head.

By the time I finally opened my eyes again, Maxie and I were the only two kids left in the stands and it was Paulie Little's turn to choose.

I crossed my fingers. *Come on, God. Just this once, okay? Just this one time don't let me be the last one picked.*

Paulie didn't hesitate a second. "Zuckerman," he called. And in an instant Maxie was on the floor with the others.

Leon Lucas slowly looked up at me, rolled his eyes, and groaned, "Wonderful. I get bucket butt."

Bucket butt. As soon as he said it, I felt the tears rush back to my eyes. But this time I managed to hold them in.

I couldn't speak, though. As Maxie and I walked out to the kickball field I kept my head bent way down like I was looking for a crumb on my collar, and I didn't say a word.

Meanwhile, Maxie started chattering away like crazy. And it was weird, you know? 'Cause even though I could hear his voice, I had absolutely no idea what he was saying.

Finally I felt him give me a shove. "So what about it?" he said. "Can I borrow the money or not?"

I stared at him blankly. "What money?"

Irritated, Maxie sucked in his cheeks. "The *dollar*, Earl. The dollar bill that you brought to school today. I forgot my lunch, so I want to know if I can borrow it."

I stopped dead in my tracks. No! Please! This couldn't be happening! Hadn't I been through enough for one morning? Did I actually have to make up an on-the-spot lie about where my dollar had gone?

"No!" I said, answering my own question.

Maxie gave me the meanest look ever. "Well, thank you, Mr. Generous," he said coldly. "Mr. Good Friend. Mr. Best Pal. It's not like I wasn't going to pay you back, you know."

He started to storm off in a huff.

"No. Wait, Max," I pleaded. "You don't understand. What I meant to say was that the money's gone already. I don't have it anymore."

Maxie raised that one eyebrow of his. "So where did it go?"

Frantically I began searching in my pockets for my Rolaids. "Uh, well, actually I gave it to someone," I managed at last.

Maxie's eyebrow refused to go back down. "Gave it to who?" he persisted.

Nervously I began mopping my face with my sleeve. "To who? You mean, like you want to know the actual person I gave it to and all? 'Cause, um, well . . . that's easy."

I swallowed hard. "I gave it to, uh . . . to . . ."

Think, Earl! Think! I screamed silently at myself. *Who do people give their money to?*

"To the Salvation Army!" I blurted out of nowhere.

Maxie looked at me like I was a lunatic. "The Salvation Army?" he repeated in disbelief. "You mean the guys with the bells and the little red pots at Christmas?"

Flustered, I began to babble. "Yes. They're the ones. See, there was this bell-ringer guy outside the boys' bathroom this morning. And when I heard his bell clang, I just automatically put my dollar in his pot. I think it was one of those involuntary reflex things. Like when your doctor hits that funny place on your knee and your leg kicks out."

Maxie was suspicious. You could tell by his face that he didn't believe a word I was saying.

Then slowly his eyes as they drifted back to Eddie's footprint on my shirt. And even though I quickly covered it up with my hand, I knew I was too late.

The wheels in Maxie Zuckerman's head had already begun to turn.

Uncle Murray

Maxie didn't waste a bit of time telling Rosie about my lie in P.E. At lunch he kept ducking behind my back and whispering secrets to her. Then later, while the three of us were walking home from school, they started giving each other these stupid signals with their eyebrows.

I caught Rosie right in the act.

"Stop that!" I snapped. "You two have been whispering about me all day, and I'm sick of it!"

Rosie turned to Maxie and nodded. "You're right. He *is* being a kaka."

"Kaka" is one of Maxie's stupid dictionary words. I think it's some kind of bird. But it sounds like something a lot worse.

"I am *not* being a kaka," I snapped. "You're

being a kaka. You're both kakas, in fact. You're the kaka twins. So there! Ha!"

Maxie tried to settle me down. "Come on, Earl," he said calmly. "We weren't telling secrets about you. Honest. We've just been trying to figure a few things out."

My muscles began to tense. This wasn't going to be good. I could just feel it.

Nervously I cleared my throat. "Like, uh, what kind of things, for instance?" I managed.

Maxie and Rosie looked at each other again. Then Rosie gave him a little nod.

Maxie lowered his voice. "Like what really happened to the dollar you brought to school this morning," he said.

A shiver shot through my body.

"But I already told you," I insisted. "I gave my dollar to the Salva—"

Rosie put her hand over my mouth. "Save your breath, Earl," she interrupted. "The Salvation Army wasn't even at our school today. I checked it out with the principal."

My hands started to get wet and clammy. I couldn't believe this! Why didn't they just mind their own business?

"Oh yeah? Well, guess what, Miss Snoopy Pooper Head?" I snipped. "Mr. Shivers probably didn't even know about it, that's all. The Salvation Army was probably just marching down the street when this guy had to go to the bathroom. And so he ran into the school for a second."

Rosie rolled her eyes. "The Salvation Army doesn't march, Earl. It's not that kind of army."

Maxie put his arm around my shoulder. "Look, Earl," he said quietly. "I know you're in some kind of trouble, okay? I even think I know what it is. But it would probably be better if you told me yourself."

His eyes drifted back to the footprint on my shirt, and he gently reached over and tried to brush it off. "It's Eddie, isn't it? Eddie McFee did this to you."

My blood went cold when I heard that. That's how mortified I was. Then I just stood there frozen in humiliation—like some fat, grotesque ice sculpture.

Finally, after what seemed like hours, I managed to walk over to Maxie's porch step and sit down. And with my head lowered in shame I heard myself whisper the horrible secret I'd been keeping inside.

"He makes me pay him, Max," I said so softly I could barely hear my own words. "I pay him a dollar a week not to beat me up."

Maxie sat down next to me. "Damn," he said in a hush. "I was afraid it was something like that. I mean, I've known there was a problem for a long time now. But it wasn't until P.E. this morning, when you didn't have your dollar, that I finally put two and two together."

After that he gave me a sympathetic pat and reached into the front pocket of his backpack. A second later he pulled out a small gray card and carefully pressed it into my hand.

I looked down.

It was the business card of his uncle Murray. The personal injury lawyer.

Suddenly Maxie's face brightened. "You can sue him, Earl," he said. "What Eddie's been doing is against the law."

His voice grew more excited. "It's called extortion. You've heard of that before, right? Extortion is when somebody forces you to pay them money by threatening to beat you up or kill you or something. And it's illegal! Get it? You and my uncle Murray can sue the pants off that creep!"

Then without warning, Maxie threw his arms in the air and yelled, "God, what a great country!"

My mouth dropped open in amazement. I stood

up. "Have you lost your mind?" I said in disbelief. "Don't you understand how humiliating this is for me? I never even wanted you and Rosie to find out. And now you actually expect me to blab it to the whole world?"

Maxie looked shocked. "But—"

"But nothing! But forget it! I told you before, I'm not telling anybody anything! If anyone finds this out, I'll be the joke of the whole school! Even more than I already am!"

I looked around to make sure no one was coming. Then I cupped my hands around my mouth like a megaphone.

"ATTENTION, WORLD! CAN YOU FOLKS IN OUTER MONGOLIA HEAR ME? I JUST WANTED TO ANNOUNCE TO THE UNIVERSE THAT I, EARL WILBER, AM A BIG FAT WIMP! AND I CAN'T STICK UP FOR MYSELF! SO I'VE BEEN PAYING EDDIE McFEE A DOLLAR A WEEK NOT TO BEAT ME UP! FILM AT ELEVEN."

After I finished shouting, I turned and started walking away as fast as I could. 'Cause I knew if I didn't get away from Maxie in a hurry, I was going to explode into a million angry pieces.

"Great, Earl! Just great!" he yelled after me. "Run away just like you always do! This is so typical! You're such a complete wimple!"

I came to a screeching halt. Oh! So now we were into name-calling! Well, two could play that game!

Furiously I spun around. *"So sue me, Mr. Big Fat Lawyer Pants!"* I hollered back.

For a moment Maxie looked like he had been slapped. Then he narrowed his eyes, hiked up his jeans, and slowly began walking toward me. He didn't stop until he was right in my face.

"Excuse me," he said dryly. "But did you just call me Mr. Big Fat Lawyer Pants?"

I looked down at him and smirked. "Yes," I replied. "That is *exactly* what I called you. I called you Mr. Big . . . Fat . . . Lawyer . . . Pa—"

Halfway through "pants" I started to crack up. I couldn't help it.

Then Rosie cracked up, too. And pretty soon even Maxie couldn't hold it in. We couldn't stop, either. We laughed until our sides ached.

After that, everything got a little easier.

"Okay. So maybe my Uncle Murray idea wasn't that good," Maxie admitted. "But that doesn't mean there's not a way out of this problem, Earl. I mean, maybe we should all just go home and think about it for a while. And on Saturday we can meet at the clubhouse and talk over some solutions. How does that sound?"

I hesitated a moment. How did it sound? It

sounded terrible! I mean, geez, just because a guy's humiliating secret is out in the open doesn't mean he wants to sit around and talk about solutions.

I stalled for more time. "Saturday, huh? Uh, well, let's see . . . Saturday . . . Saturday . . ."

Then I remembered. I had an excuse for Saturday! A real honest-to-goodness excuse that I didn't even have to make up.

"Nope. Sorry. Can't make it," I said a little too eagerly. "My mother and I have to go to a funeral on Saturday."

Rosie shivered. "Eew. Funerals give me the creeps," she said. "Who died?"

I shrugged. "I'm not sure. All I know is that some lady at work lost her best friend, and so my mom offered to drive her to the funeral."

I sighed. "Too bad it's not my funeral, right? At least that would be one way out of my problem."

Rosie punched me hard in the arm. "Don't even kid about a thing like that," she scolded.

That was when Maxie's face turned weird. I mean *really* weird. At first he just sort of squinted and began tapping on his chin. But before long his eyes were totally glazed over, like his mind was somewhere out in space, about a katrillion miles away.

After that, he began talking to himself in this hushed, eerie voice. Except the only word you could hear was "funeral." It was spookier than anything.

Next he started rubbing his hands together. Slowly at first. Then faster and faster, until he clapped real loud and kind of sprang off the step.

"Yes!" he said, punching his fists in the air. "I've got it, Earl! I think I've got an idea that will get Eddie McFee out of your life forever! Of course, I don't have any of the details yet. But I know if I put my mind to it, I can get it worked out in no time."

The next thing I knew he'd sped up the porch steps like some crazy scientist and disappeared inside his house.

Rosie and I looked at each other.

This time we *both* got the creeps.

To battle

Maxie worked on his idea almost the whole night. He said he didn't get to bed until three A.M. I believed him, too. Walking to school that morning, he looked all pooped and droopy. And he was still wearing the same wrinkly clothes he'd worn the day before.

But even though he was real tired, he still called an emergency meeting after school. "Three fifteen. My garage," he announced, yawning. "Be there."

Maxie's garage is where our clubhouse is. Except it's not really a clubhouse. It's an old beat-up '55 Chevy that belongs to his father. Still, if you lock the doors and roll up the windows, it's a pretty private place to meet.

When we all got there that afternoon, Rosie and I climbed right into the backseat. Maxie always gets the front. It's not fair, but Maxie says when you own the clubhouse, you don't have to be.

As soon as the doors were locked he pulled three reports out of his briefcase and held them up for Rosie and me to see. They were all typed up on computer paper and stapled together.

"Okay, guys, here it is," he said, handing Rosie and me a copy. "This is what I was working on all night. *The Plan*."

I looked at the printed title:

Maxie's Amazing Plan to Get Rid of
Eddie McFee
BY
MAXWELL ZUCKERMAN
(IQ 160+)

Right away my stomach started to churn. The Plan weighed a ton. I mean, geez, I didn't want to have an epic adventure or anything. All I wanted was a few extra dollars to last me until Christmas.

I tried to hand it back to him. But Maxie had already started to read. "Act One, Scene One," he began. "Earl's Note."

Note? What note? I thought. Then, against my

better judgment, I turned to the first page. And before I knew it, I was following right along as Maxie read.

The Plan was written exactly like a play—with acts and scenes and stuff like that. Even the actual conversations we would be having with Eddie were already written down for us.

Maxie has an incredible brain. Seriously. Like if Maxie Zuckerman's brain ever goes on display at the Smithsonian Institute, it probably won't even fit into one of those big mayonnaise jars.

By the time he was finished reading, Rosie's mouth was hanging open. "Wow," she said, kind of breathless. "This thing is unbelievable, Max."

Maxie puffed out his chest. "Yes, I know," he said proudly.

Anxiously he turned to me. "What do *you* think, Earl? Pretty neat, huh?"

I began to fidget. Yeah, it was pretty neat, all right. But it was a lot of other stuff, too. Like pretty risky and pretty dangerous and *extremely* hazardous to my health.

Impatiently Maxie leaned over the backseat. "Earrrll. Do you like the Plan or don't you?"

I looked at him a second. Weakly I shrugged.

Maxie's eyes opened wide. "What? Are you kidding? You mean you don't like it? How could you not like it? This plan is brilliant, Earl! It's re-markable! It's . . . it's . . ."

"Suicide," I added quietly.

Maxie paused a moment. Then, to his credit, he began to nod. "Yes, well, okay . . . I admit that some of it is a little bit scary. And it'll defi-nitely take a lot of guts on your part. But it's not like you're going to have to face Eddie alone, you know. Rosie and I will be right behind you every step of the way."

"Oh, good," I replied sarcastically. "You'll both be there to pick up the pieces of my head after Eddie busts it open like a ripe watermelon."

I turned to Rosie. "I'd bring a plastic bag if I were you. Paper will get soggy."

"Come on, Earl. Don't exaggerate," said Maxie. "Eddie's not going to—"

"Have either one of you ever been to a water-melon bust?" I interrupted. "The melon makes a disgusting splatting sound and pieces of it go flying everywhere."

Maxie sighed in frustration. "That's *not* going to happen. I'm telling you this plan will work. Once you get started, you're going to sail right through this thing as easy as pie."

"Sailing makes me vomit," I informed him.

By this time Maxie's patience had pretty much run out.

"Listen, Earl," he snapped. "This plan isn't just about you, you know. Just because you're the one with the problem right now, that doesn't mean that the rest of us don't have problems, too. I get pushed around every single day by kids like Eddie McFee. And so does Rosie. And so do a hundred other kids that go to this school."

He narrowed his eyes. "The guy's pewage, Earl. They're all pewage. And now we have the perfect opportunity to get back at one of them.

"Don't you understand?" he said, raising his voice. "This is a *war*, Earl. It's us against Eddie McFee. And we can win it! You and me and Rosie can teach Eddie McFee a lesson he will never forget!"

That's when Rosie started going crazy. "Yes!" she shouted. "Let's do it! Let's crush that egg-sucking cockroach!"

Then she and Maxie started whooping it up and high-fiving and junk.

I just watched.

I guess war is always funnest for those who don't actually have to fight.

Finally I got out of the car and plodded silently to the garage door. By the time I got there the cheering had stopped.

When I turned around, I saw that Maxie looked concerned. "We *can* count on you, right, Earl?"

he wanted to know. "I mean, you *are* with us on this, aren't you?"

For a second I just stood there staring back at him.

Then weakly I saluted.

That's what soldiers do right before they go on a dangerous mission. They turn and salute their officers.

Then they go into battle.

And no one ever hears from them again.

Extortion man

I took the long way home. There's a shortcut through Maxie's back alley. But back alleys make me nervous. And anyway, I needed some extra time to think about the Plan.

I mean, how could I even be considering such a stupid thing? If everything didn't go *exactly* right, I could end up dead!

And what about Maxie and Rosie? What kind of friends would encourage a nervous little chubby kid to risk his life like that?

A nervous little chubby kid. God, how I hated that description of myself! I sounded like a cartoon character. And I wasn't, darn it! I was just a regular guy. A regular guy with a little bit of a weight problem and a tendency to throw up in the face of danger.

"It's not fair!" I said right out loud. "A kid

shouldn't have to fight for his right not to fight! It's not even logical!"

Without realizing it, I stopped walking. Then even though I was still a block from home, I sat down on the sidewalk. And I thought about the way I looked. And the way I was. And the way I wanted to be.

And then I cussed Eddie McFee for making my life so hard. And I didn't stop for a very long time.

I can't tell you where courage comes from exactly. I mean, I know it doesn't come from sitting on the sidewalk cussing all afternoon. But still, when I got home that day, I knew that I had to try to go through with the Plan.

I called Maxie right after dinner. Since Eddie and I were scheduled to have a "little meeting" after school the next day, I needed Max to help me memorize my lines.

It took forever, too. Memorizing lines just isn't that easy for me. Especially when I know I'm going to have to be spouting them out to Eddie McFee.

But even after I finally learned them all by heart, there was still lots of work for me to do. First there was a picture to draw. And, of course, there was that note to write. Earl's Note, remember?

It wasn't going to be a pleasant note, either. It was going to be nasty. *Very* nasty.

"The nastier the better," Maxie had insisted. "It's got to make him angry, Earl. Just like the picture. They both need to make Eddie really *steamed*."

So I drew the picture. And I wrote the note. But believe me, it wasn't easy. Because writing a nasty note to a kid like Eddie McFee is like writing an invitation to your own murder.

Which, now that I think about it, was exactly what I was doing. . . .

The next morning I was a total wreck.

"I've changed my mind," I announced to Max as soon as I arrived at his house. "I can't go through with this. I thought I could. But I was mistaken."

Maxie paid no attention to me. Instead he grabbed the notebook out of my hands and started searching through my papers.

"The picture, Earl. Where's the picture?" he wanted to know.

I turned to Rosie. "I've got a new plan," I announced. "I'm going to run away and live in a foreign land."

Rosie smiled and nodded. Then she patted my hand like I was somebody's nincompoop great-grandfather.

Finally Maxie found the picture I had drawn.

His whole face lit up. "Hey! This is good, Earl. *Really* good! It's perfect, in fact!"

Excitedly he began searching for the note.

I rubbed my chin thoughtfully. "A peaceful land. Where you have to be nice to each other or they kill you."

That's when Maxie spotted the note sticking out of my jacket pocket.

"Whew! Good," he said, relieved. "For a second there I thought you didn't write it."

Quickly he pulled it out of the envelope and read out loud:

"Dear Edward,

If it's not too much trouble—and if you haven't made other plans for after school—I was wondering if you could please meet me behind the big tree in the corner of the playground at three o'clock.

If not, don't worry about it.

Love (the brotherly kind),
Earl

P.S.: Kindly come alone.
P.P.S.: Peace be with you."

Maxie glared at me.

"Does *this* sound mean to you?" he asked,

dangling the note in front of my face. "Huh? Does it, Earl? What were you thinking, anyway? I told you the note had to make Eddie furious, remember? If Eddie's not furious, the plan will never work!"

He ripped a new piece of paper from the notebook and quickly scribbled down some words. This time when he read, even Rosie looked grim.

"Ed,

   After school, dude. Behind the big tree in the corner of the playground. You and me.

   And come alone. Or ELSE!

                                        Earl"

He folded up the new note and shoved it in my pocket.

"Thank you," I said politely.

Turning to Rosie, I added, "I'm going to miss you when I'm in my new land. You've been annoying at times, but I'm still going to miss you."

Frustrated, Maxie ran his fingers through his hair. "Come on, Earl, get a grip, okay? We're going to do this thing, and that's that. Now let's go."

Then he simply turned and walked off. And Rosie walked off, too. And you could just tell by the way they did it that they thought I would automatically follow.

I didn't, though. I mean I wanted to and all. But let's face it, I was scared to death.

That's when it suddenly occurred to me that maybe this was one of those "moment-of-truth" things that happen to a person sometimes. You know, one of those critical moments in your life when you have to make a snap decision about what kind of stuff you're made of. Like whether you're going to stand up and fight. Or whether you're going to turn and run.

I closed my eyes and took a big deep breath. And within seconds I knew what I would do.

I would stand up and fight . . .

But I definitely would *not* be a good sport about it.

"OH, ALL RIGHT, YOU STUPID DOO-DOO KAKA HEAD. I'LL DO IT, OKAY?" I hollered at Max. Then I took the awful note out of my pocket and hurried across the street. And within seconds I was stationed at the front door of the school awaiting the arrival of Eddie McFee.

"There! Are you happy now, Einstein?" I growled when Maxie arrived. "Now you get to be the big wizard behind the Plan, and I get to be the dead rotting body on the playground with the worms playing pinochle in my snout!"

I knew I was a little out of control, but yelling

at Maxie seemed to give me the courage to stand there.

Just then the bell began to ring, and Rosie hurried to give me a hug. "You can *do* this, Earl. I know you can," she said sincerely.

Maxie gave me a thumbs-up sign. "Trust me. You've got nothing to worry about," he added. Which I'm almost positive is what Little Red Riding Hood's mother said right before Red set out for Grandma's.

A second later they were gone. And I was standing there all alone. Waiting for Eddie McFee. My heart was pounding so hard I thought it would come right through my chest wall.

Desperately I closed my eyes and shot up a quick prayer. *Dear God, HELP!!!!! Love, Earl.*

When I opened them, Eddie was heading into the building.

I sprang at him. "Here, McFee!" I screeched, shoving my note into his hand. "This is for you!"

Then I took off for my classroom as fast as I could.

I still don't know where I got the courage to walk to the big tree that afternoon after school. It was the scaredest I'd ever been in my whole life. Halfway there I stopped to puke. But not much came up. Just the taste of Rolaids and a little bit of Pepto-Bismol.

As soon as I got there, I turned around and saw Eddie storming toward me. He wasn't alone, either. He had brought his two giant fists along for support.

When he got to where I was standing, he took out the note I had given him and tore it into a million little pieces.

"Open up, Wilber," he snarled, holding the shreds of paper in his fist. *"Now.* You're gonna eat this."

Quickly I reached into my pocket and pulled out the picture I had drawn the night before. Then I held it up in front of his face—you know, sort of like he was a vampire and this was a cross.

"Look, Ed. Look what I've got. It's a drawing of you and me," I said in a shaky voice. "See? You're the guy in the red cape. I made you look like a superhero, sort of."

I pointed. "And there, that's me. I'm the little chubby guy you're holding upside down. See the money falling out of my pockets?"

Eddie snatched the paper out of my hands and held it closer.

"See what it says across your chest?" I continued nervously. "It says 'Eddie McFee—*Extortion Man.'* "

I gulped. "You know what that means—right, Ed? Extortion is when you force somebody to pay you money not to hurt them. It's kind of like stealing, actually."

My lip started to quiver, but I kept talking. "This is a pretty funny cartoon, don't you think? I thought maybe I'd put it on the bulletin board in Coach Rah's office. I bet he'd get a real kick out of it. Don't you, Ed?"

Eddie ripped the picture to shreds and sprinkled them on my head like confetti. Maxie had told me something like that would probably happen. We'd even prepared what I would say when it did.

I closed my eyes and swallowed hard. Then somehow I managed to get the words out of my mouth.

"I have more," I said.

Suddenly Eddie McFee leaped at me. I tripped and fell backward over the base of the tree. Quick as lightning he was on top of me, pinning my arms to the ground.

His face was as red as a firecracker. "Who do you think you're messing with?" he hissed. "Huh, you fat, sweaty little piglet? I'll kill you!"

I tried to tell him to get off of me. But nothing would come out of my throat except this dry, sick-sounding cough.

Eddie started laughing. "What's a matter, feather belly? Eddie McFee too heavy for you?" he said, bouncing up and down on my stomach.

Suddenly Rosie's voice erupted out of nowhere. "HEY! GET OFF OF HIM, YOU BIG BULLY!"

Then just as we had planned, she and Maxie started running toward us as fast as they could.

"I MEAN IT, JERK FACE! LEAVE HIM ALONE!" Rosie screamed again. "HE'S SICK!"

Eddie laughed even louder. "Ooooh. I'm scared," he said to me. "The dufus and the dorkus are coming to save you."

Rosie and Maxie grabbed Eddie's arms and pretended to try and pull him off. But Eddie didn't budge. He just kept right on bouncing.

"Rosie's not kidding, Eddie!" yelled Maxie. "Earl really *is* sick. It's serious, too. He's got very weak—"

Eddie bounced hard. A sudden whoosh of air came out of my mouth.

Maxie gaped down at me. "Intestines," he said quietly.

"Aaagghhh," I groaned in pain. My eyelids started fluttering like crazy. And my eyeballs rolled back into my head.

Eddie got off me as fast as he could. "Gross!" he hollered.

Next thing you know, my legs were kicking around all over the place like I had been plugged into a light socket or something. I tried to talk, but no words came out. Just this disgusting gargly, gurgling noise. And then some drool ran down the side of my cheek.

"Double gross!" shouted Eddie.

That's when I went limp.

Totally limp, I mean. My head rolled to the side. My eyes shut. And my tongue fell out of my mouth like a big knockwurst.

Eddie freaked out. He screamed a few cusswords. Then he took off running.

I still didn't move, though. Not for a very long time.

Finally, when everything was totally quiet, I raised one eyelid. And then the other.

It was over.

Eddie was gone.

Ruby Doober and friend

Click.
   It was Saturday morning, and I was sleeping.
Click. Click. Click.
At least I thought I was sleeping.
Click.
I opened one eye.
Zap!
A bright light flashed and blinded me!
"*Aaaaah!*" I yelled, ducking under my covers.
"He's awake," said a familiar voice.
Cautiously I peeked over the top of my sheet. Rosie Swanson was sitting on the edge of my bed. Maxie was standing right next to her with his camera pointed straight at my face.
I rubbed my eyes. "What the heck?"
"Great memory, Earl," said Max. "We told you

we'd be here at nine thirty to start taking pictures, remember? You were supposed to be all dressed and ready to go. Only right now it's after ten and you're still in bed."

"Yeah, but don't worry," added Rosie. "Your mother let us in. So we took the pictures while you were asleep. You drool, by the way."

My eyes got as wide as saucers. "You did what?" I blurted. "You mean you took pictures of me like *this*? But I was supposed to be wearing something dignified, remember? Like a suit and tie. Or my good sweater. I mean, geez, you guys, these are the grossest pajamas I have. They're the ones with the V8 juice stain down the front."

Maxie looked at his watch. "We liked the V8 juice stain," he said matter-of-factly. "Besides, we don't have time for any more pictures. You've got to get ready for the funeral, remember? You said it started at eleven, didn't you?"

The funeral. Oh geez. I'd almost forgotten about that.

I swallowed hard. "Yes, well, um, about the funeral, Max. There's something I sort of need to tell you about that."

Immediately the blood drained from Maxie's face. "Oh no. This isn't bad news, is it, Earl? There *is* still a funeral, isn't there?"

Slowly I nodded. "Well, yes. I mean, there's

still a funeral and all. Only last night my mother told me something about the uh, well . . . the dead guy . . . that might present a little bit of a problem. And I just thought I should run it by you and see what you—"

Quickly Maxie put his hands over his ears. "No. Please. Don't run it by me," he said. "I was up most of the night double-checking today's activities, and I really don't think I could take any last-minute bad news."

"I know, Max. But I still think you—"

Maxie interrupted me again. "Please, Earl. Just listen to me," he begged. "Yesterday you were so amazing that I actually got goose bumps watching you. *Goose bumps,* Earl. The really lumpy kind that don't go away when you rub them. And I think that's why I'm so edgy today, you know? 'Cause you got us off to such a perfect start, I can't stand the thought of anything going wrong. So let's keep it simple, okay? Just take the camera to the funeral, get some pictures, and forget about the dead guy."

Rosie eyed me curiously. "You're not *afraid* of the dead guy, are you?" she asked. "Because you shouldn't be, you know. I went to my uncle Moe's funeral and he wasn't scary at all. He looked exactly like he did when he was alive, except he was wearing lipstick and both his socks matched."

I just looked at her. How insulting. Why would I be afraid of a dead guy? Dead guys are so peaceful and well groomed.

"No, Rosie," I snipped. "I'm not afraid. What I'm trying to tell you guys is—"

In a flash Maxie's ears were plugged again. "I can't hearrrr youuuuu," he sang loudly.

Before I could say another word, he threw his camera on my bed, grabbed Rosie by the hand, and dashed out the door.

The funeral started at eleven. My mother and I picked up Ruby Doober at ten forty-five. Ruby Doober is the lady whose best friend had died.

"I hope it's all right that I brought my son along," my mother told Ruby when she got in the car. "He expressed an interest in coming and I think he's old enough to understand these things."

Ruby Doober nodded solemnly. Then she waved her hanky at me and blew her nose.

She pretty much blew it all the way to the funeral home. When we got there, she switched to travel tissues.

A funeral man met us at the door. He put his arm around Ruby Doober and took us to the room where her friend was.

My mother and I stayed in the back of the room

while Ruby Doober went over to the casket. I wasn't nervous being there. Seriously. I wasn't even shaking.

"Ohhhhhh, Dorothy!" exclaimed Ruby Doober. "He looks so wonderful! Just look at him! Just look at my big fella!"

Then Ruby Doober pulled a Frisbee out of this giant purse she was carrying and gently placed it in the casket. "The two of us used to love to play Frisbee together," she said, sighing. "He was a champ, you know."

Slowly my mother and I walked over to the casket. "He really does look wonderful, Ruby," Mom said.

Ruby Doober nodded sadly. "What do you think of my big guy, Earl?" she asked me.

I shifted uneasily. Since this was my first funeral, I wasn't sure of the proper thing to say. Finally I took a deep breath and cleared my throat. "I think he looks very clean, Miss Doober," I replied.

Ruby Doober looked at the body. "Yes. They *did* do a nice job bathing him, didn't they? Look. They even got that stubborn food stain off his beard."

I leaned a little closer to the casket. "In a way it's kind of spooky, isn't it?" I observed. "I mean, he practically looks alive, doesn't he? Like almost any second he could jump up out of that casket and start chasing us around the room or something."

Ruby Doober smiled. Then she reached into the coffin and rubbed her friend's stomach.

"Poor old Bobo," she said.

"Such a good old dog."

After Ruby Doober finished scratching Bobo, the three of us drove to the pet cemetery. The funeral man said he would meet us there in a few minutes.

As soon as I saw the place I breathed a sigh of relief. I had been so afraid that it wouldn't look like a regular graveyard. And a regular graveyard was critical to the Plan.

No one would ever know the difference. There were headstones on each grave. And green grass and flowers. I even saw a couple of those tiny little American flags.

The moment my mother stopped the car, I grabbed Maxie's camera off the floor and hopped out.

Ruby Doober gave me a funny look. "What's that for?" she wanted to know.

Nervously I bit my lip. Even though I had memorized my lines again, I still wasn't sure I could pull it off.

"Um, well, see, this camera belongs to my friend Maxie Zuckerman," I sputtered nervously. "And he's kind of doing this report on funerals for school. So he asked me if I would mind taking a few pictures to show how pretty and peaceful these places are. I mean, that would be okay, wouldn't it, Miss Doober?"

Ruby seemed to relax a little bit. Then slowly she turned in a circle and scanned the grounds. "You know, it *is* pretty and peaceful here, isn't it? Maybe I should have brought my camera, too."

Breathing another sigh of relief, I started walking around the cemetery, clicking pictures. I'd taken about three or four when I heard the funeral men pull up in their station wagon.

I got a shot of them setting the casket on the ground and a couple more of my mother and Ruby standing there real solemnly and stuff.

After that, we all stood by the grave while the main funeral guy read a little dog prayer.

Then it was over. Ruby Doober dabbed at her eyes and honked her nose as we walked back to the car.

"My big fella would have liked you, Earl," she said, reaching back to squeeze my hand as we drove home.

"Yeah. Well, I probably would have liked him too, Miss Doober," I replied.

It kind of made me feel bad, saying that. Sort of dishonest, you know? I mean, knowing how I had used her and all.

But then I remembered about Eddie McFee. About how he had humiliated me for all those weeks. And how at last I was finally going to get to pay him back for his meanness.

I sat up a little straighter. "I'm gonna get you, Eddie," I whispered softly to myself.

I smiled slyly. "Yup. Thanks to Bobo, I'm gonna get you good."

Dead with a capital D

Maxie and Rosie were sitting on the curb waiting for me when I got home. As soon as the car stopped moving the three of us ran straight to my room.

Rosie started asking a billion questions. "How did it go? Was it creepy? Were you scared? What did the guy look like? Was he like really, really old? Did he have on lipstick? Was he—"

Maxie reached over and covered her mouth with his hand. "Did you get the pictures? Did you explain about the camera? Did you say the part about how pretty and peaceful the cemetery was? It worked, right? The lady believed you, didn't she? Come on, Earl! Tell us what happened!"

Calmly I sat down on my bed and took a big deep breath. I mean, I know I should have been whooping it up and celebrating and all. But for some reason I just felt real calm and in control, you know? I wasn't even sweating. And my stomach wasn't a bit jumpy. It was like a totally new sensation for me.

Well, maybe not *totally* new. Sitting there, I remembered feeling the same way once before in my life. It was the first time I ever rode my two-wheeler all by myself without falling. I mean *completely* on my own—without my mother running along to catch me if I fell.

And I remembered how I got off the bike, and carefully leaned it against the garage wall, and walked straight to my bedroom. And then just like now, I sat down on the edge of my bed and took a big deep breath. And as I breathed in, my insides filled up with this magical new feeling. And I wanted to hold the air inside me forever. 'Cause I was afraid that if I let it out, the feeling would escape along with it, and I might never get it back.

Now it was happening again—only this time I knew the feeling had a name. *Confidence.* And just like before, it was the sweetest feeling in the whole world.

By now Maxie had his hands around my neck. "If you don't tell me what happened at the cemetery, I'm going to choke the life out of you! Did you get the funeral pictures or didn't you?"

I finally cracked a smile. "Did," I said, handing him his camera.

Maxie's eyes opened super wide. "Did?" he repeated in amazement. "You mean you really, really got them? They're in here?"

I started beaming. That's when Maxie came unglued. I mean it. He let out this loud squeal of laughter and jumped right on my back. And the next thing I knew, the two of us were wrestling all around on my rug.

Rosie hopped on my bed. *"Hiiiii-yaaka!"* she hollered, crashing down on top of us. The thud knocked one of my framed pictures off the wall.

Within seconds my mother was pounding on my bedroom door, screaming *"That's enough!"*

Maxie, Rosie, and I looked up. My mother had come in and was standing there in this old pink housecoat trying to open a bottle of aspirin with her teeth. It didn't take a genius to figure out she had a bad headache.

Immediately Rosie stood up and began smoothing out her clothes as if she hadn't been involved. "Oh, hello there, Mrs. Wilber," she sputtered. "That's a very lovely, uh . . . old robe-thing you're wearing."

My mother rolled her eyes.

Maxie looked at his watch. "My gosh. Would

you look at the time. Rosie and I have really got to be going."

"Darn," said my mother, holding her head. "And I was so hoping you'd stay to tea." Then slowly she turned and shuffled back out the door.

Maxie stuffed the film spool into his pocket and I gave him my last dollar to help him pay for having it developed.

As they were leaving, Rosie playfully ruffled my hair. "You did perfect today, Earl," she told me.

Maxie patted me on the back. "Yeah, but don't forget, there are still two more important things that you have to do, okay? First you've got to convince your mother to let you stay home on Monday. And second, you can't let anyone from school see you till Tuesday. You understand how important that part is, don't you, Earl? Not *anyone*."

I just grinned. I wasn't worried a bit. This time I had come up with the most perfect excuse of all time. And the little "wrestling incident" my mother just witnessed had set it up perfectly.

By the time Maxie and Rosie left I was feeling as light as a feather inside. I took a flying leap in the air and floated over to my bed. You'll just have to take my word on it. But I swear I *floated.*

*　　　*　　　*

An hour later I started screaming my head off. *"Aaaaaah! Ooooooh! Ohhhh!"*

My mother came flying into my room. "Earl? Good heavens! What's wrong with you? What *is* it?"

"Owwwww! Ouchie, ow-ow!" I cried. *"Aaaah! Aaaah! My neck! My neck! I can hardly move it! Owwww!"*

Mom sat down on the side of my bed and gently tried to move my head around.

I closed my eyes in pain. *"Aaaaaah! Don't! That kills!"*

"Okay, okay. I won't touch it anymore," said Mom. "It looks to me like you've pulled a muscle."

She frowned. "I bet you anything you did this when you were horsing around on the floor with your friends. Darn it, Earl! You know how weak your neck is! It's not like this hasn't happened before. Remember last year right before your class play? I even had to take you to the doctor."

She paused to think. "I remember he said pulled muscles don't show up on x-rays. About all you can do is take aspirin and stay quiet for a few days."

I started to nod. Then I yelled again. *"Owwwww!"*

"Don't move it!" Mom ordered. "I'll go get the aspirin bottle."

As soon as she was gone I broke into a fit of giggles.

Yes! Yes! I exclaimed silently. *I did it! I did it! For the second time in my life I've pulled off the old strained-muscle-in-the-neck trick! First the school play! And now this! You're a genius, Earl! A regular genius!*

A few minutes later my mother came back with her sweater on. Gently she started to help me sit up.

"Come on, honey. I'm afraid we've got to go to the drugstore to get you some aspirin. I took the last two this afternoon."

I felt a shudder run through my body. Had she said the *drugstore?* But the drugstore was the busiest place in town. It was right next to Happy Family Pizza Palace. And half the kids at school hung out at Happy Family on Saturdays!

Maxie's words came back to me in a rush. *You can't let anyone from school see you till Tuesday. Not anyone.*

"No, Mom! Wait!" I blurted suddenly. "I can't go there! I mean, I can't go anywhere! My neck hurts too much. Just let me stay home, okay? I promise I'll stay right here in bed and rest!"

By this time my mother was standing me up. "Sorry, but there's no way I'm leaving you home alone in this condition. What if there was a fire? You couldn't even get out of the house on your own."

"Yes, I could. Of course I could. It's my neck that hurts. Not my feet!" I wiggled my toes. "Look! They're fine! If there's a fire, I'll run like the wind."

But it was no use. My mother wasn't listening. She just handed me my slippers, grabbed the sheet off my bed, and started shuffling me out the door.

As soon as we got to the car she helped me lie down in the backseat and covered me up with the sheet.

"There. How's that?" she wanted to know.

"Terrible, that's how it is!" I exclaimed. "This is a bad idea, Mother! My neck is totally scrunched up back here, and it hurts worse than ever! I bet you anything that you've done some permanent damage, too. You're *never* supposed to move someone with a neck injury! Haven't you learned anything from watching *General Hospital*?"

My mother sighed. Then she rolled down the window so I could stretch out my legs and put my feet up.

Ten minutes later we pulled into the drugstore parking lot. Even though I was still lying down, I could see the sign for Happy Family Pizza Palace flashing next door. "I'll only be a minute," said Mom as she got out of the car. "You just lie here and be still."

Outside my opened window I heard kids talking and clowning around. They sounded close, too. Too close for comfort.

Oh geez, oh man, oh . . . God? Are you there? Listen, it's me again. Earl Wilber. Can you see me down here? I'm in the white hatchback outside Happy Family Pizza Palace. Can you see me through the roof? I'm lying down on the backseat because I don't want anyone to spot me, okay? So do you think you could help me out a little bit here, God? Like could you just keep people away from the car for a few minutes, do you think?

"Hey! Look!" called a loud voice. "I see feet!"

At first I was kind of puzzled. Feet? Someone saw feet?

I gasped. Oh, no! It was *my* feet he saw! They were still sticking out the window! How could I have been so stupid?

I froze. It was automatic. I just squeezed my eyes together and went totally rigid, like one of those Egyptian mummy guys or something.

A second later I felt a tug on my left slipper. "Hey, you in there! You with the big feet! What are you doin', dude? Are you takin' a nap or what?''

The boy yanked on my slipper again. Then he started to laugh.

"Hey, McFee! You've gotta see this! There's a zombie in here with a sheet over him!"

McFee? Oh, God, no! What kind of sick, rotten luck was this!

I can still hear Eddie's feet as he walked over to the car that afternoon. I felt like I was in one of those horror movies where you can actually hear the monster's scary footsteps plodding up the stairs. Coming closer . . . and closer . . . and . . .

Suddenly he was at the window. My eyes were still closed, but I knew he was there. I could feel him grinning down at me.

"Well, what d'ya know? If it ain't my old pal Tubbo. *Hey! Tubbo!*" he screamed. *"Hey, Tubbo, wake up!"*

I didn't flinch. I'm positive of that. When your muscles are squeezed as tight as mine were, they're not even capable of flinching.

I still don't know what would have happened if "my mother of the incredible timing" had not come out of the store at that moment.

"Hey! Get away from that car right now!" I heard her yell at the top of her lungs.

Feet scattered everywhere. A second later, the car door opened.

"Are you okay, Earl?" asked Mom frantically. "What was going on out here? Did those boys do something to you?"

I was too petrified to speak.

It was over.

All of it.

The Plan.

My life.

Everything.

When we got home, my mother helped me out of the car. "No wonder your neck hurts so bad," she said, concerned. "Your muscles feel like they're tied up in knots. Look at you. You're stiff as a board."

She was right, too. I was so tense I didn't even have to fake it anymore. Nothing helped, either. Not the aspirin. Not the hot bath. Not even the chicken soup she brought me for dinner.

Of course, knowing that I had to tell Maxie and Rosie what had happened did nothing to relax me either. Just a few hours ago I had practically been a hero in their eyes. And now I had to call Maxie with the worst news imaginable.

When I finally dialed Maxie's number that night I was a nervous wreck.

"Zuckerman residence," he answered politely.

Briefly I wrestled with the idea of hanging up.

"Hey, is this one of those sicko breathers?" Maxie asked curiously.

"No, Max. It's me," I said in a hush. "It's Earl."

I paused and added, "Earl, who—though I've known you only a few short months—has already come to discover how sympathetic and understanding you can be in times of trouble."

Through the phone cord I felt Maxie brace himself.

"What happened?" he wanted to know.

That's when it all came flooding out. "He saw me, that's what happened," I sputtered. "My mother forced me to go to the drugstore with her. And Eddie McFee was there. And he saw me."

Maxie didn't say a word.

"It wasn't my fault! Honest, Max! There was nothing I could do. My mother made me go. She *made* me! And the window was rolled down. And my feet were hanging out. And then a bunch of Eddie's friends saw them. And they called Eddie over to the car. And then he—"

Click.

That was all there was to it.

Just a little click, and the line went dead.

Dead like me.

Dead with a capital D.

Bingo

Sunday morning Maxie and Rosie were in my room again bright and early. Since my mother was outside washing the car, I'm almost positive they just walked right in the front door like they owned the place.

I was half awake when I heard it slam. The next thing I knew, Rosie was shaking me like a rag doll to make sure I was alert, while Maxie stood at the end of my bed as upset as I'd ever seen him.

In fact, he was so angry that I had ruined the Plan, he couldn't even bring himself to talk to me. So instead of speaking to me directly, he would whisper his message to Rosie for her to relay.

After Maxie's first whisper, Rosie put her hands on her hips and glared at me. "Okay, buster.

Maxie wants you to tell him exactly what happened yesterday. And he means *exactly.*"

I hate it when Rosie tries to act big.

"Please," I said. "Not the little cop routine, okay? I was awake almost all night and my nerves are shot. Besides, I already told him what happened."

Maxie sucked in his cheeks and scowled at me. He looked like a skeleton head. Then he whispered again.

"But what did you *say* to Eddie, Earl?" relayed Rosie. "Maxie wants to know exactly what you said when he came over to the car."

This time I didn't answer quite as quickly. I mean, geez, how humiliating did he have to make this for me anyway?

"There weren't any words, okay?" I confessed at last. "I totally froze up and I couldn't open my mouth. I was so scared I wasn't even breathing."

I paused. "There. Now do you have a clearer picture of the whole ugly little scene? Are you happy yet?"

Maxie looked up at the ceiling and muttered something under his breath. I think he called me a toad-eater.

That did it. I just didn't need this, that's all.

"Stop it, okay? Would you stop it!" I told him. "I mean, geez, Max, don't you think I know how

76

bad I screwed up? Only here's a big news flash for you. *I'm* the one who's going to have to eat Eddie's socks for the next few weeks. Not *you!* So if you only came over here to make me feel bad, then you might as well go home. 'Cause I can't possibly feel any worse than I do right now."

After that, I got out of bed, went to my door, and made a huge sweeping motion for them to leave.

"Thank you for your support," I added gruffly.

Then I waited. And waited. And waited.

But nobody left. Instead, the room got so quiet you could hear a pin drop. And Maxie and Rosie just kept on standing there and standing there— until the silence between us got so thick it almost suffocated me.

Rosie must have felt it, too. Because all of a sudden she bolted to the window and tried to pry it open.

That's when I heard the word "Sorry."

It wasn't loud. But I definitely heard it. And it had definitely come from Maxie Zuckerman's mouth.

It really threw me, too. I guess I just hadn't expected it, that's all.

I'm not smooth at handling apologies. Like I almost always end up saying something sappy or stupid or I knock over a potted plant. I used to pretend to boink the other guy in the eyes like on *The Three Stooges*. But I've pretty much got that one under control now, I think.

This time I did okay, too. After only a few seconds, I kind of shrugged and said, "Yeah. Well, you know. What the heck."

Then Maxie and I halfway smiled at each other and he headed for the door. 'Cause we still weren't real buddy-buddy at this point, you understand.

Only right before he left, he handed me an envelope of pictures from his jacket pocket. And with that one eyebrow of his raised, he said, "Of course, even if Eddie hadn't seen you yesterday, I guess we still would have had this little *pet cemetery* problem to deal with."

I swear you could have knocked me over with a feather when he said that. That's how stunned I was. 'Cause how could he have known? How could he have possibly—

"*Check out the tombstone,*" he said as he walked out the door.

Meanwhile, across the room poor Rosie was still trying to open my window. Only now she was using one of my bedroom slippers.

"It's locked," I said at last.

"Oh," she said. "No wonder."

"Yeah, no wonder," I repeated stupidly.

Then Rosie sort of laughed. And I sort of laughed, too. And then she casually strolled to the door and ducked out into the hall.

She didn't leave, though. I could still hear her breathing outside my door.

"Don't worry, Earl," she said softly. "It'll all work out. We'll think of something."

I smiled sadly.

That's one good thing about Rosie Swanson. She can never lie right to your face.

As soon as she was gone, I flopped back on my bed and hid my head under my pillow. 'Cause that's what you do when your future is filled with head-flushing and sock-eating.

It's very peaceful under a pillow. And dark. And if you want to, you can take deep breaths and relax your muscles and just let your brain drift all around from thought to thought and dream to dream. Brains enjoy free-floating like that, I think. It sort of gets their creative juices flowing, I guess you'd say.

I don't remember when I first got the idea that I could save the Plan. I mean, ordinarily a thought like that wouldn't even enter my head. But as I lay there under my pillow that morning, my brain eventually drifted over to the scene at the drugstore. It pictured how weird I must have looked all stretched out in the back of the hatchback, with that sheet draped over me. It remembered how I told Maxie I was so scared I wasn't even breathing . . .

And then *bingo!* Brain juices started kicking in from everywhere.

It was almost two o'clock when I snuck into my mother's room and dialed Maxie's number.

"Zuckerman residence," he answered.

"Max, it's me. Earl," I whispered as loudly as I dared. "I think I did it! I mean, I think I figured out a way to save the Plan!"

Maxie didn't answer. He was probably too busy getting one of those "Yeah, right, sure you did" looks on his face.

"Just listen to me for a second, okay?" I pleaded. "I thought of the perfect way to explain why I was at the drugstore yesterday! I mean it! It doesn't matter if Eddie saw me or not! In fact, it might even turn out better this way!"

Still Maxie didn't reply.

"Please, Max," I begged. "What do you have to lose by just listening to my idea? Come over, okay? Get Rosie and come to my house so I can explain it to you guys."

Then I hung up the phone, crossed my fingers, and whispered "please" a hundred times more.

They got to my house at two fifteen.

They went home at six thirty-five.

When Rosie left, she smiled and said, "See? I told you it's gonna work out."

This time she said it right to my face.

I didn't have a hard time staying home from school the next day. As soon as Mother touched my neck I let out a scream that could crack plaster. And since she had to go to work, she called the baby-sitter right away.

My baby-sitter lives right next door to Rosie Swanson. Her name is Mrs. Rosen from Down the Street and Around the Corner. I mean it. Whenever she phones us, she always says, "Hello, Burl. This is Mrs. Rosen from Down the Street and Around the Corner."

She calls me Burl.

She's a pretty good baby-sitter, though. She totally leaves me alone. Like if I tell her that I'm napping, she just stays in the living room and eats Oreo cookies and watches her stories on TV.

That's what she calls soap operas. She calls them her stories.

The other good thing about Mrs. Rosen from Down the Street and Around the Corner is that she makes good grilled-cheese sandwiches. She even brought one into me for lunch on Monday. But cheese is hard to digest on a nervous stomach, so I settled for four saltines and a wintergreen Life Saver.

After that, I just rolled around in my bed and watched my digital clock change numbers. I had to be in Maxie's garage at three o'clock. And the closer it got, the more pukey my stomach started to feel. That's the trouble with self-confidence. It fades in and out like a weak cable channel.

Shakily I got out of bed and started to get ready to go.

"Burl? Is that you, sweetie? Are you up?" hollered Mrs. Rosen from Down the Street and Around the Corner.

My heart started to pound. "Uh, yeah. It's me, Mrs. Rosen. I'm just going to the bathroom. Then I'm going to take another nap. So you don't have to bother checking on me or anything. 'Cause I think I'll be sleeping for a couple of hours. Okay?"

"Okey-dokle," she shouted agreeably.

As soon as I finished dressing I pulled on my wool ski mask and my Eskimo parka. My ski mask and Eskimo parka are my best disguise. Like if I ever knocked off a jewelry store, this is what I would wear.

"Okay . . . well, I'm going to sleep now," I called again. "Good night."

"Nighty-night, Burl," she called back.

After that, I shut my door and locked it. Then, quiet as a mouse, I opened my window and snuck outside. You wouldn't think a chubby guy could be that quiet. But I can be surprisingly mouselike when I try.

I got to Maxie's garage exactly at three. I was the first one there, but I knew what to do.

I pulled off my disguise and went straight to the corner of the garage. Then I sat down, snuggled back to the wall as far as I could go, and built a little fort in front of me with some boards and boxes that Maxie had left.

By this time my stomach felt like a volcano about to erupt. A volcano that not even medicine would settle.

All at once the side door opened. "Earl, are you here yet?" whispered a voice. It was Rosie.

"Over here," I called, waving a finger at her through a little peekhole I had made. "I'm shaking like crazy in here. How did everything go in school today? Did Maxie give Eddie the message to meet him here at three thirty? Is he—?"

Before I could finish, the door opened again and Maxie came blitzing into the garage with his father's video camera under his arm. He was huffing and puffing, and his hair was sticking out all over the place, like Albert Einstein hair.

He ran straight to the corner and uncovered me enough to hand over the camera.

"Quick! Take it!" he ordered, covering me right up again. "We don't have as much time as we thought we would! Eddie's coming up the driveway right now!"

Rosie gasped. "No! He can't be! I need to talk to Earl about my part some more. I thought of a couple more questions Eddie might ask and—"

Just then there was a loud bang at the door. Like someone had run up and kicked it as hard as he could.

Seconds later Eddie McFee came bursting through. I could see him clearly through my peekhole. Even though it was chilly outside, he was wearing one of those muscle shirts with no sleeves.

He didn't look happy, either. Not one teensy-tiny bit.

He walked over to Maxie and gave him a shove backward. "Okay, Zuckerman," he snarled. "What's so important that I had to meet you and your four-eyed girlfriend in this stinkin' garage?"

Maxie's face went totally pale. Quickly he reached into his jacket pocket, pulled out some pictures, and shoved them into Eddie's hands.

"Here," he sputtered. "Look at what you did on Friday."

Eddie glanced at the pictures, then raised his head. "I don't get it. What do you mean, 'look at what I did on Friday'? These are just a bunch of pictures of fat Earl Wilber asleep in his bed. So what's the joke? Huh?"

Then he put his hands around Maxie's neck and tried to lift him right off the ground.

"I asked you what the joke was, Elrod!"

Maxie's eyes were bulging out like bullfrog eyes.

Rosie pulled on Eddie's arm. She's crazy like that. "Put him down!" she demanded angrily. "How can he explain anything when you're strangling him to death? And anyway, why don't you look a little closer at the pictures. Because for your information they're *not* of 'fat Earl Wilber asleep in his bed.' "

Eddie let go of Maxie's neck and looked at the pictures one more time.

But still no light went on in his head.

"Okay, four-eyes. I give up," he growled at last. "If that's not the fatboy sleeping, why don't you tell me exactly what it is."

Rosie glared at him. "Oh, it's the fatboy, all

right, Ed. But he's not sleeping. In fact, the fatboy isn't doing much of anything at all."

She narrowed her eyes and gave Eddie McFee the spookiest look I've ever seen.

"The fatboy . . ." she said in an eerie hush, "is *dead*."

Boo

For a second Eddie's face went funny.

"What'd you just say? *Dead?* What do you mean he's dead?"

Rosie gave him her know-it-all look. "Don't you know what dead means, pal? Dead. You know . . . as in croaked, kicked the bucket, bought the farm, cashed in his corn chips. And guess what else, Ed? You're the one who did it to him! You're the one who bounced on his stomach and squished the life right out of his intestines!"

Rosie narrowed her eyes. "We saw you, too, buddy boy. Maxie and I are witnesses. We both saw you kill Earl right there on the playground. We even carried him home and put him to bed. But he didn't last long. You can't live without your intestines, you know. Intestines are some of the most important stomach junk you have."

Eddie's eyes widened. "You're crazy! I didn't squish nothin' outta nobody! The dude's asleep in this picture! That's all!"

Rosie looked annoyed. "Give me a break, Edward. Take a closer look, why don't you? I mean, I know it's a little dark in here. But have you ever seen anyone who looks that gross when they're just sleeping? He's got one eye half open. And his tongue is hanging out of his mouth like a big yellow zucchini."

Rosie made a face. "And what about that red stain all down the front of him? Do you think that's just V8 juice or something? 'Cause I've got news for you, Ed. It's b-l-o-o-d."

Eddie looked at her like she was nuts. Then he threw the pictures on the floor and headed for the door.

"You need help, girlie," he declared gruffly.

Bravely Rosie ran after him. "Okay. Fine," she persisted, holding up more pictures. "If you don't believe those, take a look at the snapshots of the actual funeral. It was yesterday afternoon, Eddie. And it was the most pathetic thing you ever saw in your life. Hardly anybody even came. Maxie and I took these pictures so you could see for yourself."

She pointed. "See that one? That's poor Earl

Wilber's mother at the cemetery. And the lady blowing her nose is his aunt, Ruby Doober."

Eddie squinted, trying to see in the dimly lit garage. "I need more light," he grumbled. Then all at once he snatched the pictures right out of Rosie's hand and started toward the window.

My heart jumped into my throat when I saw that! *No, Rosie, stop him!* I screamed silently. *You've got to keep him away from the window, remember? I told you that a hundred times. If Eddie gets those pictures near the light, he's going to see—*

Eddie's voice interrupted my panic. "Hey! What's it say on that tombstone there?"

Doomed. We were doomed.

Rosie tried to grab the pictures out of his hand. But it was too late. Eddie read the tombstone inscription right out loud: "Here lies Bobo—State Fair Frisbee Champ."

Eddie McFee grinned meanly. He was onto something, and he knew it.

Desperately Rosie looked at Maxie, who was slumped on the garage floor.

"Yes, um, well . . ." she started to babble. "Just in case you might be wondering why it says Bobo on the gravestone, it's because Bobo was Earl Wilber's *real* name. I mean, naturally he didn't want anyone to know about it. But his mother told me that he was named after his, uhhhh, his great-grandfather from England . . ."

She paused. "Bobo the First."

Sweat drenched my armpits. Bobo the First? Geez! We sounded like a clown family!

Eddie's grin got wider.

"Yeah, well, you can grin all you want to, Ed," Rosie blundered on. "But it's still true. Earl's mother told me they've got tons of weird names like that over there. She said that in England, Bobo means . . ."

She swallowed hard. *"Two bows."*

That's when Eddie stopped smiling and took a threatening step toward her. "Yeah, sure it does, geekus," he snarled. "Now tell me the one about how he was state fair Frisbee champ."

Quickly Rosie nodded. "Yup. Yes, he was," she insisted. "I was even there the day he won it."

She smiled sadly and shook her head. "Poor old Bobo. He might have been a tub, but boy could he throw that old saucer."

Suddenly Eddie gave Rosie a sharp shove backward. "Knock it off, you four-eyed geek. The joke's over. Get it? 'Cause now I've got some news for *you.* I saw the fatboy on Saturday, okay? He was in his car at the drugstore. I saw him with my own two eyes."

Then he took a few more steps in Rosie's direction and pounded his fist into his hand. "I don't know what you two dorks are trying to pull here. But you're going to pay for this. Oh yeah. You're *definitely* going to pay."

Rosie began backing up. She looked as scared as I had ever seen her.

"Quit it, Eddie," Maxie blurted suddenly. He was still rubbing his sore neck, but at least he had managed to stand. "If you're smart, you'll listen to what she's saying. Rosie and I aren't trying to pull anything. It's all true. You squished the insides out of our best friend on Friday afternoon. And if you saw him in his car on Saturday, then that can only mean one thing. You saw him after he was already . . ."

Maxie stopped and bowed his head. Then— just like we had practiced—he solemnly pointed his finger to heaven.

Eddie laughed in Maxie's face. "Oh yeah, right, brainiac. Like his mother took him shopping at the drugstore after he croaked."

"She wasn't *shopping*, Ed," explained Rosie. "Use your head. She was taking him to the . . ."

Her voice got quieter. "Well, you know, the funeral place. And she probably just stopped at the drugstore to get some headache medicine or something."

"Think about it, Eddie," Maxie went on. "I mean, just think about how Earl looked when you saw him that day. Was he sitting up or lying down? Were his eyes closed? Was he all covered up? And what about the way he was acting? Did he seem all nervous and shaky like he always did? Or was he real—"

"Stiff," offered Rosie bluntly.

Maxie continued on. "He wasn't in school today, Eddie. Call the office if you don't believe me. And he's not going to be there tomorrow, either."

Then he made his voice get spooky quiet. "That's because you flattened his large intestine with your knee, Ed. Maybe you didn't mean to . . . but you did it."

Eddie wasn't grinning anymore. "No," he insisted, shaking his head. "I couldn't have done that. I hardly even bounced on him! I was just messin' around, that's all. You two are nuts. I don't believe any of this," he said.

He did, though. You could tell just by looking at his face. Eddie McFee was beginning to believe *all* of it. Even my drugstore idea had worked!

I had just begun to breathe a little bit easier . . . when suddenly I heard it.

A knock.

A little knock at the garage door.

It was pretty weak at first . . .

Tap, tap, tap.

But then it got louder.

Knock, knock, knock.

And louder!

Bang! Bang! Bang!

Then all of a sudden the door handle turned . . .

And in walked . . .

My mother!

Oh, God, no! Not my mother! What the heck was *she* doing here? Was she looking for me or what?

My whole body went numb with fear. I mean it. I was biting on my lip and I couldn't even feel it!

Rosie began stuttering, "Mrs. . . . Mrs. . . . Mrs. . . ."

"Wilber," gasped Maxie. "Mrs. Wilber. What are you doing here? I mean, I mean—"

"He means what are *you* doing here?" repeated Rosie stupidly.

My mother looked a little bit embarrassed. "Oh, I'm sorry. I interrupted something, didn't I? I interrupted one of your little . . ."

She winked. "Meetings.

"Well, don't worry. I'll only stay a second," she promised. Then she reached into her purse and pulled out Maxie's camera.

"I just stopped by to return this to you, Maxie. I found it upstairs this morning and I was afraid it might get broken."

She paused. "It should have been returned to you right after Bobo's funeral, but—"

Maxie quick grabbed the camera and turned her toward the door again. "Yes. I know. I understand. You don't have to say another word, Mrs. Wilber. Really. I mean it. *Not another word.*"

He started to open the door for her. "Okay. Well, thanks a lot. See you."

But my mother didn't budge. Instead she turned around and gave Eddie a funny look. "You know, you look so familiar to me. I've just been standing here trying to think of where I've seen—"

Just then she snapped her fingers. "Wait a second. I remember exactly where it was," she told him. "It was outside the drugstore on Saturday. You were one of those troublemakers standing by my car yelling at my son through the window."

Eddie looked a little nervous. "Well, yeah. I mean, I was there. But—"

"But nothing," snapped my mother. "There was no excuse for that kind of behavior, young man.

No excuse at all. Couldn't you tell something was *wrong* with Earl? Did he look okay to you? He couldn't even move, for heaven's sake!''

She lowered her voice. ''The poor kid was already as stiff as a board by then,'' she added chillingly.

As soon as those words were out of my mother's mouth, Eddie's knees sort of caved in, and he slowly slumped to the floor.

''But, but . . . I didn't know . . . I mean I thought . . . I mean . . . I mean . . .'' Eddie stammered.

Mother frowned. ''Never mind. It doesn't matter what you mean,'' she said. ''It's a little too late for apologies, don't you think? Earl isn't here now, is he?''

Before my mother could say another word, Maxie took her by the arm and opened the door. Only this time he practically shoved her outside.

''Don't worry about Eddie, Mrs. Wilber,'' he said hurriedly. ''We'll take care of him for you. I promise.''

Then he slammed the door right in my mother's face and locked it.

Eddie was still on the floor mumbling to himself when Maxie walked back over and knelt down next to him.

He kind of patted Eddie on the back a little bit.

"Lucky for you that Rosie and I kept our mouths shut, isn't it, Ed?" he asked in this calm, steady voice. "But see, deep inside we both knew that what happened to Earl was an accident. I mean, we never *ever* thought that you really meant to kill him."

Eddie raised his eyebrows. "You didn't?" he asked hopefully.

Maxie shook his head. Then he stood up and casually began to crack his knuckles.

"But then again," he continued, "you know what they say, Eddie boy. The law is the law, isn't it? And so when you think about it, Rosie and I don't really have much of a choice, do we?"

He smiled. "We're calling the cops, guy."

Eddie covered his mouth with his hand. *"What?"* he gasped. *"No! You can't do that!"*

His eyes kept getting wider and wider, until finally . . . it happened! The miracle we had all been waiting for took place right before our eyes!

Eddie McFee started to cry!

Okay. Not a lot, maybe. Like there wasn't any wailing or sobbing or anything. But still, his eyes filled with tears, and they ran down his face.

Just like mine had done in the gym that day.

"No. This can't be happening!" he cried. "I was only joking around!"

Rosie folded her arms and tapped her foot impatiently. "Tell it to the judge, Rambo," she said coldly.

Eddie covered his face. There were some loud snuffling noises.

"No, man. Come on, you guys! You can't squeal on me. Please! I'll do anything you say! Just don't tell on me!"

Maxie just shook his head. "Sorry, Ed. We'd like to help you out here. But this is way too serious not to tell. Don't you agree, Rosie? Don't you think Earl would want his killer punished?"

Rosie tapped her finger on her chin. "Well, yeah. I mean, I think he would. But I suppose there's really only one way to find out for sure."

Without saying another word, she walked over to the corner where I was hiding and took the boards and boxes away.

Eddie's mouth fell open, and he started sucking in air like you wouldn't believe. Seriously. I've never heard anybody sound so shocked in all my life.

Slowly I stood up. And even though my stomach was churning like crazy, I managed to walk over to where he was standing and close his mouth for him.

Then I smiled pleasantly and said . . .

"Boo."

*　　　*　　　*

It took a little while for Eddie to understand what was happening. I mean, the first thing he did was start making those giant fists of his. But then Maxie and I explained about the video camera. And about how I'd been taping him through my little peekhole in the corner. And how his friends at school would probably get a big kick out of seeing what a funny trick we played on him.

And how he'd cried and all.

"Don't you agree, Eddie? Don't you think your friends would enjoy seeing how you fell for Earl's funny trick?" Maxie asked him.

"I think they would," chimed in Rosie. "I bet hardly any of them have ever seen you cry before, have they, Ed? This'll be fun. We can invite a bunch of them over tomorrow after school. And we can all watch it together."

Casually Maxie began to flick lint off Eddie's shirt. "That is, of course, unless our friend Ed here would like to work out a little deal with us," he said.

That's pretty much the moment when the light went on in Eddie's head. I mean, his face was still real purple. And he still had these big veins bulging out of his neck. But you could tell that he finally understood the situation pretty clearly.

"You're blackmailing me, that's what you're doing! You think you can use that stinkin'-rotten tape to blackmail me!"

Quickly Rosie jumped into the Chevy with the videotape and locked the doors. You know, just to protect our investment and all. Then she pressed her nose and mouth on the glass and stuck her tongue out all over the window.

Maxie patted Eddie on the back a moment. "Now, now, Ed," he said. "There's no reason for you to get upset. I'm sure we can come to some kind of an agreement about things. We're all very reasonable people here."

He grinned at me. "Aren't we, Earl?"

I tapped Eddie on the shoulder. "Boo," I said again.

I don't know why. It's just that all of a sudden boo seemed like the funniest word in the world. A lot funnier than when Eddie had said it to me that morning in P.E.

Eddie snarled at me. "Very funny, fatboy. Very, very funny."

I narrowed my eyes. "Oh, come on, Ed," I replied real serious-like. "You're just trying to be nice. It wasn't *that* funny."

And even though I was still scared to death of Eddie McFee, I took one more step closer to his face.

"You know what else, Ed?" I said softly. "From now on I think I would like to be called Earl."

Running amuck

I t was Wednesday morning, and I was sitting in class counting down the minutes till P.E.

Soon I would have to face Eddie McFee again. As usual, the thought of seeing him made my stomach queasy. I mean, I realized that the Plan had worked and all. But still, you can never be sure what a crazy guy like that might do. And besides, acid indigestion is a pretty big part of who I am as a person.

Even when Mrs. Mota dismissed us that morning, I didn't hurry to the gym. Mostly I just crossed my fingers and prayed that Eddie would keep his wits about him.

I read that phrase in a book one time. "Keeping your wits about you" means that you stay real calm and you don't "run amuck." "Running amuck" means charging around in a murderous frenzy. You don't actually have to run, though. Like when Eddie tried to flush my head that time? Even though he wasn't moving much, he was definitely running amuck.

Anyway, you can't imagine how relieved I was when I walked into the gym and saw Eddie and Maxie sitting calmly in the bleachers together.

Maxie was grinning. Grinning his head off, in fact. As soon as he saw me he gave me a thumbs-up sign. You should have seen the way he did it. He held his thumb right in front of Eddie's face and practically wiggled it under the guy's nose.

Eddie didn't look one bit happy about it, either. But he didn't knock Maxie's hand out of the way or anything.

Cautiously I stopped a few feet from Eddie and waved my fingers. "Hello, Edward," I managed. "How are we feeling this morning?"

Eddie glared at me. He didn't take his eyes off me for a second. It was practically like he was hypnotized.

But in spite of how scary he looked, I felt my muscles relax a little bit. And for some unknown reason I got this sudden uncontrollable urge to say . . .

"Boo."

That was all it took, too. I'm serious. Just one little "Boo," and Eddie McFee ran amuck. The next thing I knew, he had jumped out of the bleachers, put me in another one of those headlocks, and was driving me toward the cinder-block wall like I was a battering ram!

I was almost there when I heard myself begin to shout.

"HEY, EVERYBODY! GUESS WHAT I'VE GOT? I'VE GOT A VIDEOTAPE OF EDDIE McFEE! AND GUESS WHAT HE'S DOING? HE'S CRY—"

Eddie screeched to a halt so fast he made skid marks. Quickly he covered my mouth with his hand.

"No! Don't!" he begged. "I'm sorry, okay? I didn't mean to touch you."

Immediately he reached into his jeans pocket and began pulling out money. "Look! Here's all your dough back," he said, stuffing it in my hand. "Just take the money and shut up about that video, okay? We made a deal, remember?"

I opened my hands and looked down. There they were. My seven dollars. After all this time. I finally had my sock money back.

Frantically Eddie began dusting me off. "So we're okay on this, aren't we? You're not gonna squeal, right? Everything's cool between us?"

I just stared at him. *Everything's cool between us?* Had he actually said those words? Or was I dreaming?

Suddenly Coach Rah blew his whistle. "Today will be our final day for kickball, gentlemen!" he yelled, looking at his clipboard. "Continuing in alphabetical order, our captains today will be Monroe Magee . . . and Edward McFee. Monroe will pick first."

Just then Maxie came up behind me and clapped his hands in excitement. "Yes!" he exclaimed. "I *knew* that today would be McFee's turn to be captain! This is so perfect I can't believe it!"

As Maxie and I took our seats in the bleachers, my heart began to pound like a drum.

This was it.

Eddie and Monroe were standing next to Coach Rah. Monroe was scanning the stands.

"I'll take Teddy Wilson!" Monroe called loudly.

Teddy Wilson ran out of the stands . . . and all eyes turned to Eddie McFee.

But Eddie just stared at his shoes.

Coach Rah tapped on his watch. "Any time, McFee," he said impatiently.

Eddie filled his cheeks with air and let it out slowly. Then quietly he mumbled a name under his breath.

Coach Rah frowned. "What'd you say, boy? Take the marbles outta your mouth, son, and pick a man."

Eddie stared silently at his feet a few more seconds. Finally he raised his head.

"Earl Wilber," he said clear as a bell.

I swear my name echoed all the way up to the rafters. Or maybe even to heaven!

At last! After five long humiliating years. I had finally been picked *first!* And it was better than anything I had ever imagined!

You should have heard the place buzzing as I floated onto the floor that morning. I'm not kidding. People were pointing. Heads were turning. And Leon Lucas's eyes popped right out of their sockets.

Then all of a sudden there I was—standing in the middle of the gym staring up at all those faces. Faces who were going to get picked second and third and fourth and fifth. And last. But not first.

'Cause first was me.

And Maxie was second.

And from now on that's how it's going to be. It's part of the deal we made in the garage. For the rest of the year, whenever Eddie McFee is the team captain, me and Maxie are going to be his first two choices.

Eddie didn't agree to it at first, of course. But then Rosie knocked on the car window and dangled the tape in front of his face. So finally he had to.

Only here's the funny part. We don't really have a tape of Eddie McFee at all. I never even turned on the video camera that day! In the first place, I don't know how to work one of those things. And in the second place, the peekhole was way too little for a lens to fit through.

And even if it had fit perfectly, making an actual tape would've still been way too risky. Like what if Eddie had heard the little whirring noise that video cameras make? We would all be dead ducks, that's what.

But like Maxie said from the beginning, all that really mattered was that Eddie *thought* we had a tape.

Which he did.

And he still does.

And so guess what else? Death isn't in my P.E. class anymore.

There's just a two-bit bully named Eddie McFee, who wears surfer shorts and chews his nails.

And I'm Earl Wilber. Just a regular kid. With a little bit of a weight problem.

And well, okay . . .

Maybe just a smidgen of courage.

MAXIE'S WORDS

kaka (KAH *kuh*) – A type of New Zealand parrot. [p. 31]
wimple (WIM *puhl*) – A cloth for covering the head and neck. [p. 35]
pewage (PYOO *ij*) – Rent paid for the use of a pew. [p. 43]
toad-eater (TODE *ee tuhr*) – A fawning flatterer. [p. 76]